The undead ar

CHAPTER 1: HOME AND AWAY

"I can't believe it's my last day of school!" Annie explained to her little sister Thia, their undeniable beauty attracting looks.
"That means your old!" Thia told her pushing Annie's shoulder and jumping on her.
Thia still had years off school in front of her. Annie and Thia were simply breath taking, Thia was the most popular, powerful, pretty and nice girl in the school. However, Annie was stunning but not popular at all.
"I'm not old, AT ALL, thank you very much!" She replied with a dark tone. All of a sudden Annie got launched forward. Falling onto her knees almost crying, after a minute the the culprit

showed themselves... it was Annie's boyfriend trying to scare her!

Annie rolled and sat on the floor. Abruptly there was a high frequency buzzing noise, Annie leaped up and clung onto Thia, as did Ross! When the noise stopped the floor shook for all of 30 seconds. Afterwards Annie and Thia looked at each other and they instantly knew what each other were thinking. Annie grabbed Ross's lower arm and they all fled down the narrow street to the girl's small tatty house.

"PACK EVERYTHING!" Annie yelled, and Thia obeyed her every command. They packed clothes, foods, knifes, guns, water, survival kits, meds, etc.

"How do you know we'll need all this?" Ross pondered.

"Turn on the tv!" Thia replied with sarcasm while she ruffly shoved stuff in a bag.

Ross did as he was told.
'BREAKING NEWS, THERE HAS BEEN A METEOR HIT RUSSIA, PEOPLE IN THE FOLLOWING COUNTRY'S HAVE BEEN ADVISED TO STAY INSIDE: Azerbaijan, Belarus, China, Estonia, Finland, Georgia, Kazakhstan, North Korea, Latvia!'.
"But we live in Latvia!" Ross asked surprisingly.
Ross came from a wealthy family and was never made to fend for himself, for that reasoning he was never ever prepared for what was to come! Regardless Thia and Annie were brought up by there ex military officer dad, their whole childhood was a considerable boot-camp. They were taught about every natural disaster, even ones that didn't exist, like <u>zombies</u>! Therefore, they knew exactly what was happening when the ground shook.
Suddenly the tv flicked on and an emergency alert came on the tv.

"EMERGENCY, EMERGENCY, LATVIA IS UNDER THREAT..." the tv cut out.
"We need to leave!"

CHAPTER 2: RUSSIA

Thia grabbed the mounds of bags wondering how many they could actually take if they needed to flee on foot!
"WHERE ARE WE GOING!" Ross pleaded.
"Russia!", Annie explains harshly "we need to go to Russia!"
"What why?" Ross pondered.
"To look at the meteor!" Thia butted in.
Thia bounced into the back off the car in the middle seat, and Annie and Ross got in the front (because they were older).

"How much longer till Russia?" Thia grumbled.

"About 3 hours, it'll be 5 if you keep asking!" Ross replied with a giggle.
Thia huffed. The feeling of being trapped in a little box on wheels is gloomy!
After a while everything goes a bit numb and in a tired haze Thia fell asleep, then suddenly a hot-headed noise came from the from the front of the car!
"DAMN", Annie expressed angrily "we're out off gas!".
"Well... what do we do." Asked Ross, lacking common sense!
"Were do we go if we need to get gas?" Annie replied sarcastically!
"Erm, the gas station!" He pouted like a mopey dog.
Annie nodded her head reassuringly.
Ross pulled out his phone like a mind reader and looked up the nearest gas station to them!
"There's one 10 minutes away, will we make it?" He enquired.

"Yeah, we'll go there!". She snapped desperately trying to keep her tired and deprived eyes open!
It was dead as a graveyard. There was no one to be seen not a single person!
"We need to make a plan; we can't get caught being underaged driving! You go in and buy some food and drinks and everything we need, and I'll buy the gas.". Annie Explained still trying to keep her eyes open as the moon blinded her!

Thia awoke to the car screeching to an abrupt halt. They had made it to the gas station! Annie skip out of the car keeping her head down and grabbing the feisty pump to hack off the stand, to squash into her dad's old rusty pickup!
Ross skipped contently across the lengthy road to the yellow gas station! He could instantly tell that it was old, there was no doubt.

The ceiling was leaky, one of the windows was cracked, there was black mole in every corner and an old woman who looked like she was in distress! He grabbed what he needed and tried to hurry out before he caught the black plague from one of the many funguses growing off the walls.

"It's ridiculously that they make us still work in these conditions, don't you think boy," She asked fanning her face "anyway where you from, you don't look from around here!".

"Umm, Latvia!" He replied resoling his cash out of his pocket awkwardly.

"Oh, hun that place is under threat right now!" She pouted sarcastically!

"Don't remind me!" He said starting to get a bit antsy and frustrated.

"How old is your friend out there?" She asked leaning

heavily over the front desk trying to pear round to look at Annie.
"She's 22!" He lied.
"Are you sure, she looks more like 17?" She enquired death staring.
"YES, NOW STOP QUESTIONING ME!" He yelled very, very frustrated.

Ross stormed out, taking all of the stuff with him and the old women following his waddling behind.
"You guys ready to leave?" He asked getting in the car and shutting the door.
"IM CALLING THE POLICE!" the old women screamed from outside the car banging on the windows.
Thia calmly rolled down the back window and sarcastically said:
"You couldn't even bend down to pick up the phone old lady!"
Annie rolled down her window and stuck her big, fat, pointy, middle finger up at her! The old,

grumpy, agitated woman stuck it right back...

CHAPTER 3: PHONE CALL

They had been on the road for what felt like a gazillion years, but in reality, was a few hours. Eventually they came to a paltry town in Russia called 'sviyazhsk', where the meteor supposedly hit. The town was deadly hushed, there was no one in sight!

Annie stopped the car. 'I wonder where all the people are?' Thia wondered as she gazed at the old town in absolute ruins, what had happened there? Ross got out as soon as he could, sprinted round the car slipping on the corners and stood looking at IT! He had seen nothing like it in his whole life.

"What on earth is that?", Ross asked in disbelief.
Thia Sat and shrugged, she thought her dad had peppered her for everything, but she had no clue what to do next!
But then she had an incredible idea. She was calling the one person who knew everything about everything! She was gonna call her dad.

Annie hoped out the car to go stand with Ross when another rattle in the floor erupted, she grabbed his arm wobbling all over!
"My dad" Thia shrieked scrambling out the car.
"No, NO, NO, DAD!". she cried.
"THIA, COME HERE.". Ross screamed at Annie throwing his hand out for her to grab!
She pushed through the shaking and fell into his arms.
"My dad... he's still in Latvia. He's not gonna make it, he's tough but not this tough. He's

been through enough!". She cried not knowing what he had actually been through in his life. "Dad, he talks about these army people..." Annie boomed trying to overpower the noise of the earthquake.
"Oh, ye I remember, there names were something like: George and Elena!" Thia replied catching on.

Suddenly the earthquake had finished and Ross had pieced together that, the floor shaking was a meteor hitting Latvia and they needed to save the girls dad to call some army people!

Thia regained her balance and raced over to the car, hoped in the small window and retrieved a small phone with a fluffy pink case! Then her and Annie sat gracefully on the hood of the car. "Do you think he'll answer?". Thia asked unconvinced.

"Of course he will!". Annie replied reassuringly as Thia put the phone up to her ear.

It rang once, it rang twice, along with a third. Then eventually on the fourth there was an answer...

"Sweetie is that you?", A man asked on the other line.
"Ye, it's, it's me dad, are you ok?". She replied choking up some tears!
"Ye I'm fine, did you take my truck?". He chuckled.
"Maybe!", She laughed softly clutching her phone.
"I'm coming to find you guys, but you guys need to do me a favour! I need you to investigate the meteorite!". He coughed.
"Ok, wait how do you now we're in Russia?". She asked thinking he was a mind reader.
"I know everything, anyway I need to go, I'm calling my army people.". He spoke.

"Ok dad see you later!". She said proceeding to hang up the phone!

"We need to check out the meteor!", Announced Thia.
"Ok but... we should put masks on!", Remarked Annie.
She hoped off the bonnet, skipped along the little street looking in the windows of the shops!

"Ha found em'!". She sang happily as she, discretely smashed the wind with a 'window breaker' her dad gave her. With a hop she stepped into the closed shop.
"You can't just break a window then steal!", whispered Ross aggressively.
"Umm, I just did!", Chuckled Thia.

Thia picked up some blue masks from a broken wall display and handed one each to Annie and Ross, as they put them on, they strolled cautiously over to the big black rock.

CHAPTER 4: NOODLE

Annie brightly stepped forward, as almost a sacrifice, exposing herself first! Tension spiralled as she leaned forward to touch it. What would happen? Inches away she closed her eyes, thinking the worst. Then finally she touched it... nothing happened; however, she did feel a little spark of electricity corse through her vanes!
"Nothing... nothing happened?", she spluttered.
Ross trotted over and tapped it with the tip of his finger, unlike Annie he felt nothing.
"Well... umm what now?", asked Thia scuffing her dirty converse on in the mud!

"Give me a leg up.", gestured Ross trying to jump on it.
"Ok!", the girls shrugged in unison.

Ross eventually got up, and dusted himself off as there was green dust all over him, which was weird because, the authorities said there was green dust, in the last place that 'Mayer Allmen' went missing from in the next town over! Mayer was a phenomenal lass, that Annie only got to meet once at a friendly school competition. Mayer had long ginger hair, full lips and blue eyes. She was perfect and very smart!
Annie just felt bad for her Mayer's best friend: Sarah Dawn. Rumours said that Sarah had to go on anxiety meds, because she was so traumatised!

Ross sat on the top of the rock and tried to get his balance, he looked to his left and sat right beside him, was... a small, pleasant milk snake!

"Omg, look guys, I've found a wee pal.". He said picking the little snake and showing Thia (who adores animals,).

"Gimme, gimme!", she said said, putting out her hands and jumping!

"Alright!", he said bending over and leaning forward over the rocks edge, handing it over he said.
"What u gonna call him?".
She replied quickly and replied with,
"Noodle!".
Ross and Annie chuckled.
"Ok then!". Giggled Ross as he leaned back.

"Right, so what do I do?", he asked looking around as Annie fiddled with her new, little pal!

"Try make a hole with this hammer!", Annie replied reaching into her bag.
Ross obeyed and took the used hammer and put all his strength into one hard knock right on the centre top of the rock!
A large cracking came from within, and Ross quickly disappeared into the big belly of the enormous rock...

CHAPTER 5: GREEN GAS

The girls panicked as they ran up to it and thudded on the side, finally an even bigger eruption came, and the walls of the rough-edged rock came crashing down! A huge cloud of green gas arose and...
"Cover your mouths!". Annie screamed.
As the three of them got down and darted into the nearest apartment complex, a man stepped out his house and into

the gas that had wafted about! Instantly he fell to the floor and started shaking, at this point Ross covered Thia's eyed.
Approximately 6 seconds later he got up and looked about, almost like he was a toddler looking for his mum! Unfortunately, a young woman came forth and as soon as the man laid eyes on her, he ran up and bit her face. Just like the first man she dropped.

"Omg!". Said Annie being quite loud!
"Shhh, they'll hear us!". Ross shouted. Within seconds the to people were charging at the three and they had no choice but to Skedaddle up the stairs.

Round and round they went not daring to stop, after minutes of running, they came to the top and had no choice but to bang on the first door that they saw! No one answered...

They had no choice but to leap down a one set of stairs and slap the door in front of them,
"LET US IN!". they cried.

Luckily the door opened and a young blonde girl with fuzzy hair stood on the other side. She wore cute green dungarees, pretty little purple shirt, topped with some old scratched yellow converse. "Come in quick, the bad people are coming, I watch it all out my window!". She said stepping back.

They trotted in and the house was clean. Just then they heard a flush and a man stepped out a toilet on the left side of the living room.

"Umm, can I help you?", asked the man that stood in front of them.
"There are somethings out there,", squealed Thia "there coming to get us!".

"There're telling the truth daddy,", squawked the little girl, "I saw them out the window!".

"Ok clementine, this is for the grown ups to discuss!". Said the man getting on his knee and comforting the wee girl.
"I'm Annie, this is Ross, and this is Thia, somethings have happened and it's not good so my father, who is lieutenant colonel in the military! And he's on his way to this very place!". She said being direct.

"I'm Jeff, does your father know what's happening?", he asked!

Just then there was a series bangs on the door on the door and they didn't stop.
"Go to the bathroom lock the door and I'll get my guns!". Screamed Jeff, throwing clementine to Ross. The kids obeyed as Jeff ran into the other room!

The bathroom was pleasant enough however it was a bit chaotic!

As Thia slammed the door, they heard gunshots and growling. Annie thought of the worst as it all went quiet.
"I'll go first!". Ross said slowly turning the doorknob.

He stepped out quickly turning to check down the hall, then kept creeping along through to the living room.
It was empty! Jeff was infected by whatever the two people had, and many other would be soon.
"I'm calling dad!". Announced Thia grabbing her phone.

"I'm going to Scotland and you and the others are going to meet me, you guys have let out something that's going to ruin the world!". Her dad said breathing heavily, after he hung up.

"We're going to Scotland...".

CHAPTER 6: EARTHQUAKE два

Looking out the window, Ross decided that the best way to get down to the car was by distracting the undead people was by moving their attention to something else, therefore chucking a rock as they all sprinted down the hall.

**Making it too the car wasn't easy, there were more of them! Thia had to jump on the roof of the car and slid through the window.
"Thia give me your phone, I'm calling dad,", said Annie. "I'm asking him where we need to go in Scotland!".**

"He didn't answer, just left me a postcode, TD46BH!". She putting down the phone, while her eyes

started to droop. Why would he leave them a postcode?

After 2 hours into the trip over Clem started to dance in her seat.
"You alright hun?". Asked Ross who was sitting next to her, while this was asleep, and Annie was driving!
"I need to pee!". She explained wriggling about and tapping her hands in the seat.
"Alright babes, I'll stop at the closest gas station!". Said Annie whilst she shook Thia to try wake her up.

"I wanna do something fun!". Gurgled Thia.
"Like what?". Grumbled Ross
"Grass sledging, whilst we still can, like dad said this "bug" will change the world from ever!". She snickered.
"GRASS SLEDGING!". Screamed clem.
"Why not, we'll stop there too!". Shrugged Annie.

Suddenly Annie turned the car. "Shoot I nearly missed the turn!". She huffed.

"I'll take you to the toilet, while they get some snacks, and some food for noodle!". She said turning off the engine.
"Who's noodle?". Giggled clem. Thia pulled him out her pocket and snickered to herself.
"He's so cute!". She joked.

In the shop there was a tv and it had broad casting the report about the new virus, they called it 'redead'.
"That's quite a good name,", Thia "although I could come up with better!". She chuckled.
"Oh ye, like what!". Taunted Ross. Thia stayed quiet and her checks red.
Ross strolled of laughing to himself.

"Your total is £2.65, are you paying cash or card?". Asked the cashier.
"Cash!". Replied Ross scrounging through his pockets.
"It's wild about these redead things, isn't it?". She said glaring up at the tv screen.
"Ye so crazy!". Thia snorted.

Outside clem and Annie were waiting for them.
"I've just got of the phone with dad, he's panicking!". Ranted Annie.
"What was he saying?". Asked Thia.
"He says we're gonna meet up with his friends, and their kids...". She moaned.
"So we have to try survive this his total strangers, that's so great!". She sarcastically smiled.
"But I'm really surprised because he said they all lived in Russia, just in different towns. He also said that the chances of us seeing them on the streets and not

knowing it was them is high!". she growled.
"But didn't dad grow up with these people?". Asked Thia.
"Yep!". Replied Annie sourly, whilst she turned round and started the car.

It took 2 hours to get to grass sledging, however Thia and clem slept the whole way.
Strolling in clem held Ross's hand and jumped about.
"Are you excited!". Asked Annie looking down at her.
Clem nodded.

The lady at the front desk was really rude, however they were there to have fun one last time, so they ignored it!

"I wanna go with Annie, I'm scared!". Screamed clem as her and Ross flew down the massive slope, the hind restlessly tugging her hair. Just after Annie and Thia rushed down with rapid speed!

Annie stood up at the bottom of the slope as she was getting a phone call.
"Hello?".
"Hi, is this Annie steward?". Screamed a voice on the other end!
"Yes, what can I help you with?". She asked with a lump in her stomach.
"You rat, I'm gonna die and it's all your fault, I hope your whole family dies!". Said the voice as the phone cut out.
"Who was that?". Asked clem.
"Just a spam caller!". Replied Annie, not wanting to frighten her, Annie knew she couldn't tell anyone about this. If she felt this bad about what they did, how would Ross feel?

"Excuse me miss, the park is closing, you must leave!". Asked one of the workers.
"Ok, sorry!". Grumbled Annie.

Walking out clem went red. She was burning up.
"Clem why are you so red and hot?". Asked Ross
"Don't worry this happens a lot. I have high blood pressure!". She grumbled softly.
"Oh, are you alright to keep going?". Asked Thia tilting her head and looking sympathetic.
"I'm fine!". She stomped.

Getting in the car Thia decided she wanted to play some games in tho car. So, her, Annie and clem played some games, however they quickly got bored and put on some wild music. It took several hours to get to there. And when they did, they were were greeted by Shawn (the girls dad).
"My girls!". Shouted Shawn whilst pushing their heads into his chest.
"I'm so happy your safe!". He said getting emotional.
Clem didn't care, and strolled in the house.

"Wow little lady, where you going!". He chuckled as he ran over and grabbed her.
"That's Clementine, but she goes by clem, her dad was the third person to get infected!". Grumbled Annie with her arms crossed.
"Oh?". He replied with a straight face.
"Well, we better get inside!". Shouted Shawn with a taunting but pleasant look on his face.

The house was dark, bleak, however it was homely.
"I lived here with your mother!". He said picking up old photographs.
Thia never met her mother, she died giving birth, nevertheless, Thia saw a strong, independent woman. Thia and Annie are only 2 years apart (this's 13 and Annie's 15).

"We need to get you lot kitted out.". He said hitting his thigh and chuckling.
"What do you mean?". Asked Ross.
"I need to give the lot of you weapons, maybe not you clem, but you get what u mean!". She said walking up the stairs as they followed him.

The room they were taken to was even bleaker than downstairs, and it was filled with cabinets. Shawn strolled over to one of the cabinets, opened it, and pulled out a small handgun. As he rubbed his dirty, rough hands over the smooth grip, and strolled up to Ross.
"For you,", he said. "Put it in your waist band!".
Ross obeyed, slipping it into is elastic waist band, the cold metal handle rubbing against his thin skin.

"And for my littlest baby, a nice punk deluxe grip!". He said blowing the old dust off it.
Thia went red and twirled her foot as she stood, an awkward smile appearing on her face every so often.
"And lastly, my oldest girl, Annie!". He pulled out a plain black revolver and handed it to her with a proud look on his face.

Walking out the door they all started joking and giggling.
"Hop in peeps!". Shouted Shawn as he jumped into his convertible, 7-seater pickup truck. Clem and Thia smooshed into the two back seats as Shawn got into the driver's seat, Annie and next to him and Ross blooped himself in the back.

The drive to the army headquarters that they were going to, was short and quick. They wasted no time.

"We need to be careful going through this town, it's quite dangerous!". He said reading a pamphlet.
"What do you mean, dangerous?". Enquired Thia, looking puzzled.
"It's just a rough town, and it's called Galashiels, one of my good friends still lives here she's the here.", He croaked as he smiled at the sign with the town name on it. "This is where I did my cadet training!".

As the pulled round the corner, the army headquarters in sight. When suddenly... another earthquake happened.

CHAPTER 7: LOCKOUT

Thia put her hands over clem's head and held her tight, whilst Ross tucked down in the footwell of the backseats and Shawn

grabbed Annie and shoved her head under his shoulder. After a few seconds the worst had passed, however, in the second that their eyes were shut, a new meteor at accumulated 60 yards in front of the car.
Shawn raced out, his curiosity getting the better of himself. "MASKS, EVERYONE, MASKS!", he bellowed sprinting back to the car and grabbing his own mask.

Effortlessly hoping on top of it, he stamped as hard as he could, and he had just enough power to totally smash the rock and fall inside.
"YES, YES YES, there here!". He announced breaking down another side of the rock.

Silence echoed as everyone wondered about what was in the meteor. As they all strolled over with what looked like small perfectly, circular balls, that were off, pale greens colour!

"What the hell are they?". Asked Annie tilting her head and curiously picking it.
"NO, don't touch.". He scampered looking at them with delight on his face!
"Quick we need to get them incubated in the headquarters.". He sniffed, bounding forward in an agile walk. A walk so fast that clem had to jog to keep up!

The army building was tall and dark with the occasional light on; however, this was just the outside Thia couldn't picture the inside, and even if she did, she knew it would be far from her imagination! So staying quiet, well trying to, she and the others followed Shawn into the building.

The gas had started to spread, and you could hear wales and bangs coming from outside. None of them dared to look. As they found the lockups, where they hold all the highly dangerous

criminals, luckily there was no one in.
"Put the ac down all the way!". He said pinching a ring of keys and trotted over to the farthest away cell, and put the the 'eggs' in the cell and locked the door behind him.
"We'll come back in twenty minutes and see how they've changed!". he said putting a timer on his watch!

As the walked out they heard a noise come from upstairs! Shawn took a minute and looked up as if he was judging what to do next, to clem horror, they kept going onwards. They reached a hollow metal staircase. As they ascended Clem's heart pounded out her chest, and just as they came to a large room, Shawn stopped.
"There's someone coming, quick we need to run this bit!". He murmured bracing himself.
Ross picked up clem and they dashed into this dark silent hall.

Everything was going well, Shawn and Annie made it across however, the safety barrier came down before they could make it.

"NO, NO, NO!". Cried clem climbing of Ross's back.
It- its ok!". He scrambled giving her a hug.
"It's ok, just go downstairs take two lefts and you'll come to a ladder, down stop, don't ever stop. I'll meet you on the roof!". Dragging Annie up the stairs.

Thia turned, looking around as she remembered something.
"m-my dads map,", ranted Thai, clem and Ross looked puzzled.
"My dad gave me a map of this place!". As she scrambled in her pocket, she pulled out a dusty, stained, piece of paper with words on it.
"Down the stairs left, left, ladder!". She repeated.
"This way, we need to go this way!". She springily shouted,

bounding of to one of the many hallways.
Walking around, there were so many new noises emerging from the outside chaos.
"Oh no,". Frowned Thia, "we took a wrong turn!". A tear rolled down her face.

They were now in a large hall and a word came from behind them.

As the three kids turned round, they see two groups of people that looked just as beaten up as they did, Ross realised 'this is real, it's actually happening!'

"Julia, is that you?". Asked a man from the second group of people. I'm- I'm Thia, Julia was my mother!". Sniffed Thia.

"Was,". Gasped a woman from the first group, "wha- what do you mean, was? No, she can't, she can't be dead?". Screamed the women falling to her knees as the young women comforted her.

This was it the world changed in that very moment, there was no going back, they were surrounded by people that didn't know, however seemed to know them...

Printed in Great Britain
by Amazon